LITTLE MISS STUBBORN
and the Unicorn

Roger Hargreaves

Original concept by
Roger Hargreaves

Written and illustrated by
Adam Hargreaves

EGMONT

Little Miss Stubborn is, as you might imagine, the most stubborn person in the World.

She is as stubborn as a mule.

She is as stubborn as a herd of mules.

Once she has made her mind up about something, then there is no changing it.

For example, last week she decided to go on a picnic.

The weather forecast said it was going to rain.

All her friends said it was going to rain

It was raining when she set off for her picnic.

And it rained on her picnic.

But she is so stubborn, she did not even take an umbrella with her.

The day after her soggy picnic, a very excited
Little Miss Chatterbox telephoned.

"You'll never guess who I spoke to this morning,"
exclaimed Little Miss Chatterbox. "I was walking
through the wood, the one down by the river, when
I saw the most extraordinary sight! You'll never guess
what it was. It was so exciting! I hardly know how
to tell you. You just won't believe it, but it's true.
I saw it with my own two eyes. It was incredible.
I met a Unicorn!"

Little Miss Chatterbox can take rather a long time to
say what she wants to say.

"Nonsense!" snorted Little Miss Stubborn. "Unicorns don't exist."

"But …" began Little Miss Chatterbox.

"I don't believe you," interrupted Little Miss Stubborn and she hung up.

The next day, Little Miss Stubborn met Mr Bump.

A very excited Mr Bump.

"You'll never guess what I bumped into this morning. I bumped into a Unicorn!" he announced proudly.

"Nonsense," snapped Little Miss Stubborn. "Unicorns don't exist!"

"But …" began Mr Bump.

"But nothing. I don't believe you," said Little Miss Stubborn and she walked away.

She passed by Little Miss Sunshine who was in her garden.

"If only you had been here half an hour earlier," called Little Miss Sunshine. "There was a Unicorn here in my garden and I rode on its back!"

"Nonsense!" exclaimed Little Miss Stubborn. "Unicorns don't exist!"

"But …" began Little Miss Sunshine.

"No buts, I don't believe you!" interrupted Little Miss Stubborn.

And so it carried on.

It seemed that everyone had seen a Unicorn.

Mr Tickle had tickled a Unicorn.

Little Miss Greedy had fed a Unicorn.

And Mr Muddle declared that he had seen a unicycle.

Although, of course he meant to say a Unicorn.

And would Little Miss Stubborn believe any of her friends?

Of course not!

Not for a moment.

Little Miss Stubborn turned down the lane, through a gate into her garden.

And there, clear as day, helping itself to an apple from her apple tree, was a Unicorn.

"Hello," said the Unicorn. "I have been told that you do not believe in Unicorns."

"That's right," said Little Miss Stubborn. "Unicorns do not exist."

"So what am I?" asked the Unicorn.

"You," said Little Miss Stubborn, walking up to the Unicorn, "are a horse!"

With which, Little Miss Stubborn reached up and grabbed the horn on the Unicorn's head.

But to Little Miss Stubborn's great surprise, the horn was real.

The Unicorn really was a Unicorn.

"Well?" said the Unicorn. "What do you have to say now?"

Little Miss Stubborn screwed up her face and crossed her arms.

"I don't believe in Unicorns!" she said, and stamped her foot.

Stubborn to the very end.